Soldier's Farewell

Soldier's Farewell

A Western Story

Johnny D. Boggs

FIVE STAR
A part of Gale, Cengage Learning

Detroit • New York • San Francisco • New Haven, Conn • Waterville, Maine • London

Five Star Publishing, a part of Gale, Cengage Learning.

Set in 11 pt. Plantin.

Printed on permanent paper.

LIBRARY OF CONGRESS CATALOGING-IN-PUBLICATION DATA

Boggs, Johnny D.
Soldier's Farewell : a western story / by Johnny D. Boggs. — 1st ed.
p. cm.
ISBN-13: 978-1-59414-689-3 (hardcover : alk. paper)
ISBN-10: 1-59414-689-6 (hardcover : alk. paper)
I. Title.
PS3552.O4375S57 2008
813′.54—dc22 2008032988

First Edition. First Printing: December 2008.
Published in 2008 in conjunction with Golden West Literary Agency.

Printed in the United States of America
1 2 3 4 5 6 7 12 11 10 09 08

For Henry W. Allen,
who I wish I had known,
alias Will Henry, alias Clay Fisher,
who I know pretty well

Prologue

July 25, 1865

"And Cain talked with Abel his brother," the verse in Genesis reads, "and it came to pass, when they were in the field, that Cain rose up against Abel his brother. . . ."

For four years now, that bit of Scripture has been echoing through my head. Four years, better than four, actually, I've envisioned myself playing the rôle of Cain, justifying premeditated murder.

I am not my brother's keeper. Nobody could keep a tight rein on Julian Munro. Not me. Not even Pa.

Four years of hatred, abomination for my own flesh and blood, four years of torment. Four years watching this miserable stagecoach station in the middle of nowhere turn to dust, watching me mutate into fugitive and vagabond. Four years waiting for a war to end, waiting for my older brother to dare show his face—never once accepting the fact that he could very well have been slain by some enemy's bullet, by grapeshot, or fever, or . . . maybe . . . a broken heart.

No, for four years it has been written in my own broken, blackened heart that it would be me who rose up against my brother.

". . . and slew him."

Hard words, I've been told. Bitter words. Wrong words. Too much for a boy not even 17.

"The devil owns this place," Tori pleaded with me. "Always,

it is cursed. It kill you, too, if you no leave. Get out, Smith. Get out! Please, for God's sake, you must go, for your own sake!"

She had been crying when she said all that. The last time I saw her, close to a year and a half ago. Strong words, perhaps even the right words, coming from a young girl's mouth, but, like me, she had been forced to grow up quickly. Lieutenant Julian Munro had seen to that.

If you're reading this note stuck inside this diary, you have arrived at Soldier's Farewell. Not much to look at, is there? You're at North Latitude 32°, 21 minutes, 23 seconds, West Longitude 108°, 22 minutes, 16 seconds—we learned that from Pa—or, once, what seems like a lifetime ago, 33 1/2 hours from Franklin to the east and 41 hours from Tucson to the west—Mr. John Butterfield had chiseled those numbers into our heads. That had been during the running of the Overland Mail Company along the old Ox-Bow Route, from Tipton, Missouri, all the way to San Francisco, California, twice-a-week (each way) mail and passenger service covering 2,800 miles in less than 25 days.

The Ox-Box's no more. The war ended that, left Pa busted. Once this place bustled four nights a week. Now. . . .

Well, it's like Pa used to tell us: the only sure bets in this country are wind and dust. Which is all you'll find now. That, and crumbling ruins. And the dead.

You're 1,051 miles from Fort Smith, 460 1/2 from Fort Yuma. And 6 inches to Perdition. Pa always said that, too.

Pa—he was born Wallace Conner Munro, but most folks called him Conner, or Mr. Munro—used to tell us lots of things. He even said, fairly often, that a Scot from Boone County, Missouri, by way of South Carolina and Mississippi, could depend on his sons. Julian proved him wrong.

Reckon I did, too.

According to the family Bible, my name is Innis Smith

Munro, but folks have always called me Smith, which came from Ma, Ainsley Smith Munro. She died three days after I was born, but Pa never blamed me for her passing. Nor did Julian, 11 years my senior. I've heard stories about fathers and siblings hating the child whose birth led to the mother's death, but that was never the case with us Munros. No, that hatred burned itself into our blood a dozen years after Ma was called to Glory.

Pa often said Ma would have thought of me as God's blessing, what with, between Julian and me, there being three stillborns and two girls who never lived more than a month. Every once in a while, Pa'd even call me a blessing.

Blessing.

Or maybe, like Tori Velásquez called this place, a curse.

The diary tells the story. I'm leaving it behind for whoever happens across it. In this accursed place, though, I would not tarry. Not that there's anything to keep anybody here.

Smith Munro

November 23, 1860

Friday. Eastbound brought this leather-bound diary, a birthday present from Julian. It's a week late, but that's all right. Julian's been busy, and Pa was glad to get a letter. I'm too tired to really write anything, though. Not even sure what I'm supposed to write. Stage was 20 minutes late, passengers irritable, though not as prickish as Pa was with Marco Max, the jehu.

"Mr. Butterfield was always preaching that 'nothing on God's earth must stop the U.S. Mail,' but you always test God, sir," Pa thundered at him, "and Wells, Fargo, and Company, and especially me!"

To which Marco Max said he was too tuckered out to listen to Pa throw worser a conniption than his sainted mother used to throw back in Vermont.

Mighty tuckered out myself. Maybe I'll think of something later to write down.

November 24, 1860

Slumgullion for breakfast, then work. Pa read Julian's letter again. Wish my brother had told me what a boy's supposed to write in a diary. A big Tobiano kicked Benjamin Jakes, that reprobate of a hand Superintendent Giles Hawley saddled us with, in the leg. The sorry cuss swore he'd kill that jenny as soon as he could walk again, but then Pa practically nailed his hide to the wall. Told Jakes he'd do no such thing, that he—Pa,

I mean—had been breeding mules for nigh 20 years and Sweet Ainsley's the first Tobiano he ever seen.

She is a pretty mule, too. White legs, brown face with a snip, almost perfect brown ovals on her flanks, and mane and tail of two colors. Must be a tad taller than 16 hands. Only one like her that I've ever seen, but I ain't but 12. I like my mule, Ivanhoe, better, even if he is smaller and only a sorrel. But he's mine. Sweet Ainsley, she's Julian's.

"Sweet!" Jakes fired back at Pa, sweat from pain peppering his face. "Think that mule's sweet? It nigh broke my leg. I don't think I can walk."

"That figures." Pa didn't have much use for Jakes, lazy as a cur, always finding a way to get out of chores. Wouldn't surprise me if Jakes walked behind Sweet Ainsley apurpose.

"Smith!" the old man called out to me, practically begging. "Can you help this ol' hand to his bunk? My britches is 'bout to bust." He was rubbing his leg, which had swole up something fierce. Maybe it was busted after all.

"Smith's got work to do," Pa said flatly. He had disappeared into the stone-walled stable.

"Well . . . but. . . ." Ben Jakes almost sobbed. "How can I get to my bunk, Mr. Munro? I be bad hurt."

"Crawl," Pa told him.

November 25, 1860

Slumgullion for breakfast again. Pa watered it down even more so it'll last longer. Mighty sick of that poor-tasting stew, but it'll be the same for dinner and supper, if we get supper. Westbound's due at 8:30 tonight. It's Sunday, but there ain't no Sabbath for the Overland Mail Company, although Pa, as has been his habit long as I can recollect, prayed and made me recite a verse before breakfast.

" 'Jesus wept,' " I said. "John 11. Verse 35."

Pa's dark eyes bore through me. Julian used to do that fairly often because it's the shortest passage in the Bible. Sometimes Pa'd let him get away with it. Other times, he'd threaten a whipping with his razor strop. Wasn't sure what he was going to do to me this morn, especially with them eyes so cold, but he finally looked at his plate, and told me: "Pass the stew."

Will write more if I get time.

November 26, 1860

Didn't get time last night to write no more. Stage was on time, early in fact, but had to work harder because Ben Jakes remained off his feet. Fact is, that leg of his is black and blue as tarnation, still pretty swole up. Eastbound should be back around midnight, if it's on time, and Ben Jakes won't be no help. Seldom is. Still, Pa's been in a good mood. So I asked him what I was supposed to write in this here diary that Julian give me.

"What do you want to write?" he asked me.

"I don't know."

"What have you been writing?"

I shrugged. "Just that Sweet Ainsley kicked Ben Jakes. . . ."

"Mr. Jakes. He's your elder, Smith, worthless piece of Texas trash that he is, you still call him Mr."

"Mr. Jakes. Just that he got kicked in his leg."

"That's good. You should have written that Sweet Ainsley had kicked him in his head. That would have been better."

I stared. Started to say—"But he wasn't kicked in the head."—only then Pa must have seen the look on my face, and he just laughed, laughed real hard, knocked the hat off my head, and tousled my hair. He ain't done that but once or twice since we left Boone County, Missouri.

"Your mother kept a journal," Pa said at last, and his face warmed the way it always did when he started talking about

Ma. Warm, but sad. If you can picture that. Maybe you got to see it. I ain't the writer like Mr. Scott or Mr. Dickens.

"Ainsley must have filled ten of those books, maybe more. I never saw the use, but it's good practice for a boy your age. Not much book-learning to be had out here."

"Did you ever look at what Ma wrote?"

He shook his head. "Oh, she'd read a passage to me now and again. And when we left Port Gibson, we somehow lost one of her diaries, and she pitched a fit over that. Feared somebody would read it. 'Isn't that what it's for?' I asked her, and, by grab, that stirred her up like a hornet. 'No, Conner Munro, it most certainly is not!' she informed me. 'A diary is for the person writing in it. To record her innermost thoughts. Her wishes. Her hopes. Her dreams. . . .' "

Pa stopped. All of a sudden, he just stared at his boots. I started to say something, only decided against it. I'm only 12, but I ain't stupid. At last, Pa looked up, real quickly, then stood and turned away. "I guess," he said as he walked outside, "that's what you write. Whatever you want to, really. What you think. What you want."

"Like talking to God?" I asked.

"Maybe. I wouldn't really know."

Same day, 11 o'clock

Nighttime. Change of teams is in the stable, ready to go. That's how Mr. Butterfield told us to operate back when he run this show, and how Wells, Fargo, & Company still wants it run. We harness the mules together in the stable, then when the stage arrives, while the jehu and conductor are helping unhitch the wore-out team, we lead the fresh mules, already hitched together, to the Celerity coach. That's so a mule don't bolt away and cause a delay. The Overland don't like delays.

Pa don't neither.

I bet most boys my age ain't drinking coffee at eleven in the evening, but the Eastbounds don't get here till midnight—if they're on time—and I have to lend a hand, even if I don't draw no wages. But I'm with Pa. That's good enough for me.

Still not sure what all to write. Wish I had Ma's diaries to look at, but they ain't here. I asked Pa about them, but he just shook his head. Said he left them in Missouri with all of Ma's other things.

That ain't the truth, though. Julian told me. He's older, you see, eleven years older than me, so, once, right before he went off to West Point, he told me that right after Ma got called to Glory, when they wasn't sure I'd live much longer my ownself, that Julian woke up one night—probably as quiet as this one, least, that's how I picture it—and he got out of bed. Aunt Bertha, the midwife who had been tending to me since Ma's passing, was asleep, too. So was me. Only Pa and Julian was awake. My brother looked outside, and he seen a big fire, seen Pa. He said Pa was crying, but I don't believe that, not for a second. Must have been smoke in Pa's eyes is all. Anyway, Julian told me Pa was burning all of Ma's dresses and things. Julian couldn't never figure out why. Said he didn't dare ask. Don't blame him.

Reckon Pa burned her diaries that night, too.

November 27, 1860

Reading part of *The Three Musketeers* by Alexandre Dumas after we got the Westbound stage off—no delays, no problems, talked a bit to a boy from Memphis, said he was 13, going with his stepmother to join his pa at his spread in California east of Fountain Spring—it occurred to me that I ought to put some history in this diary.

Pa runs the Overland Mail Company station at Soldier's

Farewell in New Mexico Territory, or, as a passel of folks have labeled this southern strip of desert, Arizona Territory. Some folks don't call it Soldier's Farewell, but *Los Penasquitos,* but don't ask me what that means. Not sure I even can say it right. One time, I heard Bartolomé talking to Alyvia Velásquez, and Bartolomé, sweeping his hands at the surroundings, called it, *El Lugar Que El Diablo Posee.* I asked them both what they was talking about, because I know *diablo* means devil and that pricked my interest a mite, but they just pretended not to savvy nothing I said.

This is what they call a timetable stop on Division IV, running from Franklin, Texas—which many folks are starting to call El Paso—all the way to Tucson, where Superintendent Hawley has his headquarters.

Time's important everywhere on the Overland, and real important at a timetable stop. First thing Pa bought, before we left Missouri, was a fancy American Watch Company key-winder that must have set him back a right smart of money. Solid gold, and that pocket watch keeps time right near perfect, though Pa can guess the time almost as good just by looking at the stars or sun.

This is hard country. And lonely. Full of Apache Indians, though they have let the stagecoaches and stations alone, excepting when they want to steal mules. That's why Pa, when he was in San Antonio, stopped by the H.D. Norton & Brothers store and paid cash money—which is all the Norton boys would take—for a pile of those newfangled Colt revolving pistols and some other weapons. I ain't got to shoot one yet.

Our nearest neighbors would be other Overland employees at Barney's Station 19 miles west of here, or Ojo de la Vaca 14 miles to the east, over toward Cooke's Spring, where there's another station. We're a supper stop for the Westbound stagecoaches (Sundays and Wednesdays), but just change teams

quick as we can on the Eastbounds (Tuesdays and Fridays). Emmett Mills works at Cooke's. Him and Julian got to be pretty good pals during the short time they knowed each other. Emmett's 19, I think.

We work here with Mr. Benjamin Jakes—I've already wrote about him—and a red-bearded guy named Fletcher. Once, when Fletcher first started working for Pa, I made the mistake of asking him what his full name was, and he just spit out tobacco juice, and answered: "Fletcher's all there is."

I was only 9 at the time, and I barked back at him to quit funning me, to tell me his full name, and that's when Pa grabbed my collar, jerked me into the stable we was building, and give me a lesson in manners. "You don't ask a man his name, Smith," he told me. "You don't ask him where he came from. If he wants, he'll tell you. If he says his name is Fletcher, his name is Fletcher, and if that's all there is, that's all there is. Mr. Fletcher."

Fletcher's all right. He don't say much, and I do call him Mr. Sometimes I pretend that's his first name.

We also have a Mexican named Bartolomé, who I wrote about briefly before, and he's a good hand with mules, which is practically all we run on this part of the Overland. Even Pa says Bartolomé—he ain't much older than me, so I don't have to call him Mr. or *señor*—is one of the best hands with mules he has ever seen, and that's mighty high praise, coming from Pa.

The only other neighbors we have, who ain't drawing time from the Overland, is the Velásquez family. They live on what's known as Walnut Creek, due northeast of here under the shade of Cow Springs Mountain. That's a joke. There ain't no walnut trees on that creek, 'cause it ain't much of a creek, nor have I ever seen a cow there, and that mountain sure don't throw out much shade. I'm not sure it's even bigger than Soldier's Farewell Hill.

In fact, there ain't a whole lot of shade nowhere in this country. About the tallest things that grow are these yucca cactus plants, although there's some nice cottonwoods over at Cow Springs. But here it's just the yuccas and some brush and a ton of dust.

I like the Velásquez family. They feed us real good when we visit, or they come see us. They make this flat bread called a *tortilla,* which I'd never had before I come to New Mexico, and beans—they call them *frijoles*—seasoned with chile peppers. Never ate nothing like that in Boone County, but those *frijoles* are something good. Good and hot. And the *tortillas* are tastier than the crackers or cornbread Pa serves passengers at the station. At least the *tortillas* ain't got worms in them, which is more than I can say about those crackers. And they ain't stale. Pa'll serve the cornbread till it's harder than one of them stones in the stable. Once, I heard Marco Max tell Pa he'd pinch the braided hair off a large cent coin. Not sure what that meant, but Pa just snorted, and Little Terry got a good chuckle out of it. Little Terry rides as messenger, or guard, on most of Marco Max's runs. His brother, Big Terry, and a fellow called Donnie Oh are the other regular jehu and messenger.

I think Julian's always been sweet on Alyvia, the oldest Velásquez daughter, the one who was talking to Bartolomé in Spanish that time I just wrote about. The other girl is Tori—that's short for Victoria—she can be a nuisance, being maybe a year older than me, but sometimes I'll dance with her when we have a fandango or something because Tori and Alyvia—and *Señora* Dolores, of course, their ma—are the only females in this part of the country. Their father's name is Alejondro. Pa says *Señor* Velásquez knows this territory better than anybody, and *Señor* Vee, which is what most of us call him, helped us build this place when we first got here, a little more than two years ago.

I'll write about how a Missouri boy came to Southern New Mexico Territory next chance I get. Pa's calling, and Pa ain't one to let me bide a minute more'n I have to.

More later.

Same day, 3 o'clock

My name is Innis Smith Munro. I wouldn't write that if this diary was just for me, but Ben Jakes, when I was bringing him his dinner, he said he'd heard I was writing in a diary, and then he went on to tell me that was a good thing, so my grandsons would know what life was like when I was a boy.

Ain't got much use for Ben Jakes—Mr. Ben Jakes, I mean—but what he told me sure got me to thinking. Of course, when I asked him if he kept a diary, he just snorted and said he didn't read nor write but heard about what other folks done. I also thought about Pa, if he had burned all those diaries Ma kept along with her clothes and such, how he might have robbed her grandchildren—and me and Julian, even—of knowing what she had seen and done and heard when she was growing up. Even after she had grown up. Besides, I already wrote before that I'd tell how a Missouri boy come to Soldier's Farewell. So here it is:

I, Innis Smith Munro, was born on November 13, 1848, at our farm in Boone County, Missouri. My brother, Julian, he was born in Camden, South Carolina, on March 12, 1837. I'm copying this here stuff from the Bible, which Pa keeps on the table in our house, which is only a 12×14 stone shack next to a 70×40 foot stable with stone walls 10 feet high. The mules live better than folks working at Soldier's Farewell, but, I reckon, they're probably more important in this desert.

Ainsley Abigail Smith was born in Camden, South Carolina, on July 16, 1818. Ma died on November 16, 1848, in Boone County, Missouri. Pa was born in 1816. No date. No town given. He married Ma on April 2, 1835, in Camden. There's nothing about my grandpas and grandmas, but there is a sentiment:

To Conner and Miss Ainsley,
"Who can find a virtuous woman? for her price is far above rubies."

All my best on this blessed occasion,
Wade Hampton III

I've heard Pa mention Wade Hampton before. He and Pa used to go bear hunting in Mississippi, where Wade Hampton had a plantation. He also had a bunch of land and slaves in South Carolina. Pa never owned no slaves. I'm not sure if he believes in what I heard some passengers call "the South's peculiar institution"—but bear hunting with Wade Hampton, that's how Pa discovered Mississippi, which is where the Munros moved to in 1842. The last I'd heard about Wade Hampton, he had been elected to the United States Senate. Reckon Pa hunted bear with a right famous fellow.

Ma, Pa, and Julian lived in Port Gibson, and that's where Pa joined the Mississippi Rifles about the time the war broke out with Mexico. Pa's still got the rifled musket he carried in that war. They call it a Mississippi Rifle. Pa says he ain't never had anything that shot so true. He says when I get a tad bigger, he'll let me shoot it, but, right now, all I can shoot is an Allen & Thurber Pepperbox, a little .31-caliber pistol he bought in the Nortons' store in San Antonio when he bought all those Colt pistols and rifles. Pa taught me how to shoot and load the Pepperbox, in case we get attacked by Indians or something.

It was with the Mississippi Rifles—Pa said the official name was the 155th Infantry Regiment but everybody called them the Mississippi Rifles, and that's about all he's ever spoke about that war—where he served under Colonel Jefferson Davis, who later became Secretary of War and is now also in the United States Senate. Pa knew some really important folks, didn't he?

It was in the war, at a place called Buena Vista, that Pa got bad hurt. Never talks about it, though, and I've learned it's best not to ask him, even though I'd sure like to hear all about that gore and glory. He come back to Port Gibson, and moved the family to Boone County, Missouri, and that's where he started raising mules. Which is where I was born. He often says all his mules was born in Missouri.

One time he said that I reminded him that Julian was born in Camden, and he let out a real belly laugh at that one, then admitted he had to correct himself. "I had one mule born in South Carolina, the rest"—and he'd knocked my hat off—"were sired in Boone County."

Mr. John Butterfield called Pa the best mule man in Missouri, but Pa said, as he'll often tells folks—"It takes an ass to breed a mule."—but Mr. Butterfield, being a pious fellow, didn't laugh at the joke. Pa went on to say, serious-minded, that, no, there was lots of good mule breeders in Central Missouri, and he allowed how David Hickman and Nathaniel Leonard, not to mention Doc Rollins, were some of the greatest jack-stock men you'll ever find. He also said Eli Bass, just down the pike over toward Ashland, was better than Pa'd ever hope to be.

But Mr. John Butterfield hired Pa anyway.

By then, you see, Julian got an appointment to the U.S. Military Academy at West Point, New York. That sure made Pa and me proud. Didn't hurt that Pa knowed Jefferson Davis and Wade Hampton, Mr. Davis being in the U.S. Senate again and Mr. Hampton at that time serving in the South Carolina General Assembly. So in 1854, Julian set off for West Point. He said he'd be a "plebe"—whatever that is. By the time he graduated, 15th in a class of 27, in 1858, me and Pa had settled in New Mexico Territory.

More chores. Will finish later.

Same day, half past 8 o'clock

Pa won't like it none if he found out I was still writing in this diary and not sleeping—Westbound stage comes in tomorrow night, and Ben Jakes still ain't walking—but Pa and Fletcher shared a mite of corn whiskey after supper, and he's snoring on his bed.

I was 8 years old when Congress approved this mail contract to Mr. Butterfield and his associates. Congress agreed to pay $600,000—by jingo, that be a right smart of money—and Mr. Butterfield had a lot of work to do. Stagecoaches carrying mail, and some passengers, would leave twice a week from Missouri and California, and those stagecoaches had to get there in 25 days or less. That's 2,800 miles, meaning the stages would be running day and night.

I remember Pa telling how Mr. Butterfield first explained everything to him. I wasn't there. Pa had taken a matched set of buckskin mules—buckskins are fairly uncommon, too—to some place in New York, where he had sold the pair to this rich man, then gone to visit Julian at West Point.

"We shall put stations at intervals of 20 miles or so. Quick stops, but also a stop for breakfast and supper, but those will be no more than 40 minutes."

"You'll kill your driver," Pa told him.

"The jehu will go only 60 miles, the conductor no more than 120."

Pa still had his doubts. "Can't be done, sir."

"Can be done, sir," Mr. Butterfield said. "And will be done, by Jehovah. I've heard about your work with mules, seen your mules, and I have been told mules, not horses, are much better suited for the Western territories."

"That's true. They're sure-footed. Strong. Reliable."

"And Jesus Christ rode a mule."

"Wasn't one of mine." Pa had grinned. He said Mr. Butterfield didn't find much humor in the remark.

They haggled some, then Pa come back to Boone County, telling Mr. Butterfield to have his man look him up, and he'd sell him some mules. Mr. Butterfield didn't waste no time.

I reckon Pa had no notion of actually leaving Boone County till the Overland Mail Company man came to buy some mules. Lots of mules. They got to talking, and Pa glanced over at the little fence around Ma's grave, and suddenly started hounding the Overland man with questions about the route and what all it was going to take to get this business going.

"250 stagecoaches," the man had said, "1,800 horses and mules."

"And men?"

"1,200. Superintendents, guards, blacksmiths, clerks, drivers, stationmasters."

"All them positions filled?" Pa had asked.

November 28, 1860

The Velásquez family come over after breakfast. I wasn't paying no mind, reading some more of Mr. Dumas, when Tori snuck up from behind and yanked my hair. It's pretty long. Pa ain't got around to cutting it lately.

I turned around—that smarts, you know—and almost cut loose with a string of oaths anybody who has worked with mules has heard plenty of times.

"What are you doing?" I yelled at Tori, and then her ma started firing out some words in Spanish that I couldn't keep up with, and Tori looked down, muttering—"Sí, sí."—and lifted her eyes, her head still bowed, and said: "*Lo siento,* Innis Smith Munro."

I didn't say nothing, just glared at her. Tori's 13, but sometimes she acts like she's 3. She was wearing a colorful dress. Usually I see her in muslin and sandals, and her hair had been washed. I could smell the yucca soap she'd used. Yucca's a cactus that grows in these parts. I don't know how they make soap out of it. Pa uses lye soap. Makes me use it too, when I get around to taking a bath. Lye soap don't smell good, but it'll clean you down to your bones if you ain't careful.

Señor Vee checked in on Ben Jakes, and reported to Pa that the swelling was starting to go down, that he didn't think nothing was broke, and that Mr. Jakes would probably be up and around in a day or two.

"If not," *Señor* Vee said, "you should send him along his way."

"I should do that anyway," Pa said. He wouldn't, though. Not many folks wanted to work for the Overland in this here wasteland, and Mr. Jakes done some work, sometimes.

Then *Señora* Dolores brought out victuals she had brung us for dinner. "Roast lamb and fried potatoes," Tori told me, and we started setting up our table outside. Even Ben Jakes hobbled out of the little bunkhouse inside the stables, and we had us a regular feast.

"Have you heard from. . . ." Alyvia—she's 16, I'm guessing—looked kind of sheepish. "*Señor* Julian?"

Pa and *Señor* Vee exchanged looks, and then Pa smiled and told me to fetch the letter Julian had wrote. He read it aloud. Just now, I pulled that letter out from the old *Graham's Magazine* somebody left behind, which is where Pa keeps all of Julian's letters, and that ambrotype of him in his cadet uniform that he brung Pa. I'm copying down Julian's letter. It ain't much. Julian never wrote long letters, but he's busy.

15 November 1860

Pa:

I take pencil in hand to let you know that I am in good

health and wish the same for you and Smith. Looks like I've forgotten Smith's birthday again, but at least I'm not too late, so I'm sending this diary. He needs to practice his letters and grammar. Tell him I don't expect to find this diary in the privy next time I'm out there. [Pa mumbled through that part when he read it aloud to the Velásquez family, but still blushed a mite.] *Tell him to write.*

We're finally back at Fort Tejon after spending months chasing Paiutes on our "punitive expedition" under command of Captain James H. Carleton for what happened at Bitter Springs on the Salt Lake Trail. I'm not sure Paiutes murdered those two white men there. I think they might have been killed by white men, but second lieutenants do not question their orders. Heard from George Bascom. You remember him? We were in the same class at the Academy, though he's older than me. We got a pass together when you came to West Point that time after selling that rich hotel man those buckskin mules. George is stationed at Fort Buchanan with the 7th Infantry. I wrote him that I've finally seen the elephant. It got hot, but, as I've said, I am unscathed, though burned a dark brown by the sun. If you think Soldier's Farewell is brutal, you should spend months in the saddle in the Mojave Desert fighting Paiutes.

I'm sure you've heard the talk of war back East. All the officers are discussing it at Fort Tejon.

I have to close for now. Wish you and the little kid well. Tell him Happy Birthday from me.

Your loving son,
Julian Munro
2nd Lieutenant
1st U.S. Dragoons
Fort Tejon, California

I'd heard Pa read that letter twice, but now he didn't sound so excited, and I realized it wasn't that happy a note. Maybe it was only then that I first heard, I mean understood, most of the words.

"What does 'see the elephant' mean?" I asked.

"He's been in battle."

"Really?" Now that excited me.

"I will thank the Blessed Virgin that he is safe," *Señora* Dolores said.

Pa told her: *"Gracias."*

"Boy's right about the talk of war," Ben Jakes said as he filled his mouth with lamb and potatoes. "That's all I been hearin', and I reckon I'll be makin' my way to Texas to fit with 'er if the North keeps provokin' us."

"You do that," Pa whispered, so low I think I was the only one who heard him, me being closest to him.

"What war would that be?" I asked. "With the Paiutes? The Apaches?"

I don't know rightly what a Paiute is, but I know all about Apaches. As I've wrote before, we live right smack dab in Apache country, and a few of them have taken a fancy to our mules. Either Pa, Bartolomé, Fletcher, or Ben Jakes will be on guard duty. I've told Pa I could stand a turn, but he ain't yet give me a chance.

"No," Pa answered.

I was about to ask him—"Well, who then?", getting a mite irritable, I was—but *Señora* Dolores blurted out that this was to be a happy celebration, and that she had not been informed that I had a birthday recently, so she told us all to forget any gloom, that Lieutenant Julian remained safe and healthy, that it was a beautiful day in November, and we, too, had our health.

So we ate up. Except Pa. Reckon he was off his feet some, but he still sat at the table with us, sipping coffee, pretending to, anyhow, and smiling, only I didn't see much enjoyment behind his eyes.

Same day, quarter past 9 o'clock

Westbound stage came and went. I'd hoped *Señor* Vee would stay and help with changing teams, but the Velásquezes can be peculiar folks, being Mexicans, I reckon, and *Señora* Dolores wouldn't hear of being here after dark. They sometimes act like this place is full of haunts and such, but I never seen no ghost.

Still, we fed the Westbound passengers our leftovers, so those travelers got more for their dollar than most folks get.

I forgot to finish my story about how we all got here.

Once Pa and the Overland man started talking about the positions, the Overland man told Pa to get to Tipton when he got a chance and to talk to this fellow named Lauer, that he was the man to see about hiring as the fellow at our house was just buying mules.

Well, next thing I knowed, we had sold most of our mules and breeding stock to Eli Bass—keeping some of our best animals—and was bound for New Mexico Territory. That was in the spring of 1858. Pa and me met up with Superintendent Hawley in Franklin, Texas, where they hired some men, and we headed west. We crossed the ferry over the Río Grande north of Fort Fillmore, and followed the old Fort Webster Road—which wasn't that old, really—through the pass near Cooke's Spring, and lighted at Soldier's Farewell.

"How'd this place get its name?" I asked Pa.

Pa just stared. We'd never seen no country like this, that's certain sure, and never felt a sun as hot as this. That's saying something, because I'd sweated out a ton of water back in Missouri.

"It's the end of the earth," Pa said.

That's been a joke betwixt me and Pa. I'll ask him how this place come to be called Soldier's Farewell, and he'll think of some answer. I'm right certain he knows. What I don't know is if he's ever give me the truthful answer, but I suspect he's just telling me nothing but falsehoods. It's a game. Julian and I have a game, too.

We'll look at the clouds, and imagine they're something other than clouds. Once, I pointed to our cabin in Missouri. And Julian spotted a dun mule. Another time, he pointed to what he said was North Barracks, but I couldn't tell what he meant. Don't know a thing about North Barracks.

Julian's only been here once. That was after he was graduated from the Academy. He come here waiting for his orders, which he got a short while later. So he had a hand in building this place, and changing teams and feeding folks and taking a turn standing watch so Apaches didn't run off our mules. Hear tell they eat mules. They better not eat Sweet Ainsley, or, worser yet, my mule Ivanhoe. We didn't finish the station and stable till that November. By then, Julian was off to California as an officer in the dragoons.

The first stagecoaches started coming in mid-September of '58 when there wasn't nothing up yet but a tent. It was something hectic when the wagons would arrive afore we got everything built. Ain't slowed down since.

November 30, 1860

Didn't have a chance to write nothing yesterday or this morning. Eastbound came through on time. Wind's blowing something fierce, and you should see the clouds over the mountains to the west. Wish Julian was here. I'd tell him I see the face of Poseidon, the darkest part of those clouds being the Greek god's beard. Bitter cold. You wouldn't think how cold the desert gets, but that wind makes it unbearable. Maybe it'll rain.

December 1, 1860

Ben Jakes is up and around, complaining though. I sure miss the Velásquez crew. Even Tori. Well, mostly I miss the grub they brung. We're back to jerked beef, wormy crackers, maybe bacon, but mostly slumgullion stew.

December 2, 1860

The Westbound came through tonight, and there was a lot of talk at the supper table. I want to think about it, make sure I remember everything right, before I write it all down in this book.

It's Sunday. For my breakfast Bible verse, I surprised Pa. I read Matthew 7:24, where Jesus says: "Therefore whosoever heareth these sayings of mine, and doeth them, I will liken him unto a wise man, which built his house upon a rock."

Lot of rocks here.

December 3, 1860

Reread all that I've wrote so far. Still trying to think about the conversation from the previous day before I put it down.

They say there's almost no water along the Overland Trail between Texas and Tucson. The spring at Soldier's Farewell isn't far, in a ravine northeast of here. Before the dragoons came through in '56, travelers camped north of the peak near Hawk Springs. Anyway, when we got here, my job was to dam up the spring we use now. I bet I hauled two tons of rocks, putting calluses on calluses on my hands. But when Pa and Superintendent Hawley looked at my work, they said I was worth twice the wages I was drawing. They was funning. I ain't drawing no wages.

Then Pa, he knocked the hat off my head, pulled me close to him, and said to Mr. Hawley: "Smith's a blessing, Giles."

To which Mr. Hawley said: "I warrant he is. You done fine work, son."

To me, that was better than any wages from the Overland Mail Company.

Same day, half past 4 o'clock

Fire's going in our house. Bitter cold. Wind hasn't slacked a whit. Nary a drop of rain.

Let me describe my home. The door to the house, and gate to the big stables, face southwest. Fireplace is in the north corner, but I think it draws most of the heat from it. Usually that ain't so bad, because most days it gets blistering hot. Inside the stable, next to the gate, there's a 10×12 room, and that's where the other men live. The wall is nothing but rock slab, but it stands 10 feet high. Pa yelled at me twice when we was building it, telling me not to climb on that thing, that I'd break my neck, and usually Pa don't have to tell me a thing more than once, but that wall, when it was just being built, that was hard for a boy to resist. So Pa had to yell at me again a few days later.

He didn't have to tell me no more. By jingo, I could hardly sit down for a week after the second time.

If there ain't no dust storm, you can see the beginnings of the Burro Mountains. When the Westbound leaves, that's where it's heading, first to Barney's Station. But the stage don't go into the real mountains. *Señor* Vee says that's some real spectacular country.

The nearest mountains are called the Langfords, but, if you ask me, they don't amount to much. Rough country. Not much but creosote and saltbrush here, and them yuccas I've wrote some about, though higher up, *Señor* Vee says, you'll find an oak and some mountain mahogany.

It was from the Big Burros that Pa and *Señor* Vee traveled when we was building the station to fetch a flagstaff. They brung back a Ponderosa pine they'd chopped down, and went to work on it, turning it into a flagpole that got erected right outside the bunkhouse in the stable.

Mr. Butterfield had said Overland stations were part of the U.S. Mail, and thus should be flying the American flag. Pa agreed, but the first stage hadn't run yet, so when he and *Señor* Vee put up that flagstaff and unfurled the colors, it wasn't to please Mr. Butterfield or Superintendent Hawley. No, that was for Julian.

Don't know where that flag come from. Sure is a ragged-looking thing.

The flag was flying two days before Lieutenant Julian Munro come home. That was July 23, 1858.

December 4, 1860

Tuesday. The Eastbound came through at half past midnight, 30 minutes late. Wind still howling.

December 5, 1860

Thinking of Julian, I'll get back to my story about when he first came here.

I got to raise the flag this morning. Usually Pa does it, but D.N. Barney, the director who runs the change station west of here, showed up for coffee and confidential business talk.

Back to Julian and two years ago:

We knowed he was coming, only wasn't sure when, and he just showed up that July morning with a couple of carpetbags and a high-stepping horse, looking like a real gentleman in that uniform, except for his excuse for a mustache, and proudly showing us his "sheepskin"—that's what he called the diploma that proved he was a graduate of the United States Military

Academy. That and his ring.

Pa, well, I never seen him so proud. Figured he might up and bust. He told us that his grandma and grandpa were the first Munros to even learn how to read and write, and he never expected to see one of his own children go and get a real education, and serve all of our United States.

"I'll be in the dragoons," Julian said. "They'll send orders directly."

Well, Pa, he insisted we throw a *baile. Señor* Vee brung down his family, and *Señora* Dolores cooked and cooked, and, by jingo, I never seen such food. Emmett Mills come down from Cooke's. That's when he first met my brother, and Emmett and Julian took to each other like brothers. They was always off hunting, or racing. Kind of made Alyvia Velásquez jealous. Don't reckon I cared much for Emmett hogging my brother like that, neither.

That's when Pa presented Julian with his gift. You should have seen the look in my big brother's eyes when he first saw that jenny. Like I say, a big Tobiano like that ain't a mule one sees every day.

"The Army provides mounts, Pa," Julian had said, "and I do own a horse."

"Yeah, and I've seen that horse you paid hard money for, Jules," Pa had said with a snort. "But I'll keep her here for you. She'll get better treatment than with your dragoons."

"I'd appreciate that. What are your rates to stable her?"

"We can work something out. I hear the Army doesn't pay much more than John Butterfield."

"Sounds like you just want a reason for me to come back here."

Pa was staring off toward Mexico. He started to say something, yet didn't finish, then looked at Julian standing there in the wind, him having to hold that cap on his head with both hands.

"That's what I want," Pa said. "That's payment enough. You come back."

I didn't understand all of that. Not then. Not until maybe when Pa read that letter to the Velásquez family a few days back, and I realized that being a lieutenant in the 1st U.S. Dragoons might not all be glory. Pa had "seen the elephant" down in Mexico with the Mississippi Rifles, and he had almost gotten himself killed at Buena Vista. It struck him that Julian, his oldest son, my only brother, could right easily get killed out West.

Julian wasn't here long, and, like I wrote, he spent most of that time with Emmett Mills, though he'd sneak down to see Alyvia a time or two, probably more often than that. Finally the orders came, and we all had to say good bye. He was to proceed to Fort Tejon in California.

"That's just down the road," Pa said.

"Then y'all come visit," Julian told us. He looked off into the desert, suddenly grinned, and said: "I guess this is how this place earned its name. A soldier's farewell."

"Not farewell," Pa said. "This is just. . . ." He whispered something in Spanish.

"Till we meet again." Julian nodded.

We shook hands. I used to like it when Julian would kiss my cheek good bye, but finally I got too big for that stuff, and I liked it more when he'd shake my hand. Made me feel like a grown-up. That morning, I offered him my hand, waiting for that firm shake, but Julian knelt down and pulled me close to him, held me the longest time, and, thunderation, he up and kissed my cheek.

"Jules," I cried out, wiping his slobber off my face, "I'm way too big for that!"

"My apologies, sir," he said, and turned to Pa. They shook hands, and then Julian did the strangest thing. He pulled Pa close to him, and they embraced, and he hauled off and kissed Pa's cheek. You never seen Pa's face turn so red.

Julian had a horse, a muscular bay stallion—Pa didn't care much for him, though—which he'd saddled. And he swung up on top and tipped his cap at us.

"You ain't named that jenny Pa gave you," I told him.

"That's true," Julian said. "She'd feel lost without a name."

I was betting he'd name that mule Alyvia, but my big brother fooled me.

"Sweet Ainsley," he said.

Pa's face softened. "That's a fine name."

Then, Julian rode off.

Ain't seen him since.

December 8, 1860

It's been a few days since I've written. But I've heard more talk about the troubles back East, so now I think I can write about that supper-table conversation I overheard back on the 2nd. It went like this:

One of the passengers was a tall gent in a flat-crowned straw hat who hailed from Indiana. Name was Reagan. Said he had business in San Francisco. The other man, wearing spectacles that he was constantly wiping with a rag, come from Mississippi. I don't know where he was bound to or what his name was, and, like Pa had learned me, I knowed better than ask no questions. Other passengers kept quiet, just wolfing down their slumgullion or slurping coffee.

I wasn't paying attention to what those two gents was saying, just filling coffee cups, running the soles off my boots, until the Mississippi man slammed his fist on the table, and shot up real quick.